—

The
CHRISTMAS
MOUSE

For Matthew - my Christmas Day boy

The CHRISTMAS MOUSE

*Stephanie Jeffs
and Jenny Thorne*

TAMARIND
BOOKS

Out of the corner of his eye Oscar saw the black cat jump towards him. Without stopping to think, Oscar ran up the garden and darted into the roots of the thick hedge. His heart was beating fast, his breath like steam in the cold evening air.

He waited, trying to catch his breath, and watched the large flakes of snow fall gently to the ground. He pricked up his ears and listened. All he could hear was the thump of his heart beating.

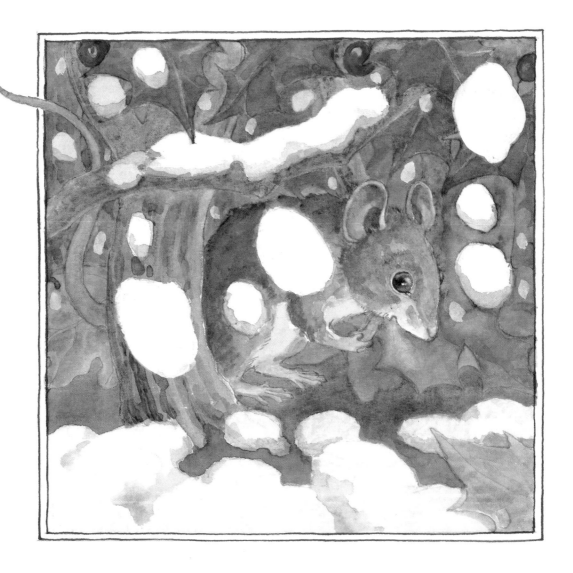

Slowly Oscar moved out of his hiding place, looking carefully around him. A snowflake landed on his nose sending a cold shiver through his little body. As he looked down the garden, he saw his hurried footprints only half visible under the growing layer of snow. There was no cat to be seen.

"That was close!" thought Oscar, with a gulp.

He crept out into the open and paused, sniffing the air and looking from left to right.

Without warning the cat pounced again, catching his tail with her claws. Oscar ran.

He flew up the garden, leaping up the stony bank towards the big house, too frightened to look back. "Hide!" thought Oscar desperately. "I must find somewhere to hide!"

Then he saw it – the perfect place. With all his remaining strength, Oscar jumped as high as he could. He tumbled and fell, and then lay still, warm darkness all around him.

Oscar lay in the toe of the boot and waited. Gradually his heart stopped thumping and his body stopped shaking. He shuddered when he saw the small pin prick made in his tail by the cat's claws.

He tried not to think of the cat stalking and waiting for him. Was she waiting for him now? Was she sitting watching the boot, tail slowly moving, whiskers taut and alert, tongue licking hungry lips?

Then in the stillness Oscar heard a sound. He froze.

"Blackie!" called a voice. "Here Blackie!"

Oscar shuddered. He began to shake and tears welled up in his large round eyes.

"What have you been doing?" said a cross voice. "You're soaking wet!" The cat purred.

"No, you don't!" said the voice firmly. "I'm not having your wet paws dirtying the house! Not tonight! You can sleep in the shed."

The cat miaowed sulkily. But Oscar heard the door close firmly and the footsteps disappear.

"Alistair!" called the voice again. "You've left your boots in the porch. You'd better bring them in. It's snowing hard outside."

Oscar scrambled to the toe of the boot as it swung high in the air. The boot fell and toppled over. Oscar remained still and waited.

How long he waited he did not know. The house was warm and he began to feel sleepy. All he could hear was the slow tick-tock, tick-tock, of a clock.

Oscar was sure that danger had passed. He crept out of the boot, feeling the warmth of the carpet on his feet.

He made his way along the skirting-board in the dark. Then he stopped. There was a crack in the wall, a crack large enough for a small mouse!

As Oscar pushed, the wall seemed to give way...

... and he found himself in the most beautiful place he had ever seen!

The dying embers of the fire cast an orange glow around the room.

On the walls hung shimmering pictures, dozens of them, with smiling faces, steaming puddings, choir boys, sheep and shepherds.

On the ceiling hung bright balloons, and silver chains were looped around the walls like a large, bold spider's web.

But there, in the corner of the room, was a wonderful tree. Oscar had seen many trees before, but never one quite like this. It stood in a large red container, its branches covered with delicate silver strands hanging like icicles. And at the foot of the tree lay many different shapes, all covered in pictures, ribbons and bows.

Oscar moved closer and stared. At the very top there was a beautiful figure, dressed in white. Lower down he saw a star, some candles, and tiny parcels. There was so much to see, he didn't know where to look next!

Suddenly something at the bottom of the tree caught his eye. "Well, I never!" he said aloud. "There's a picture of a mouse!"

He was staring at a parcel wrapped in red paper and decorated with red ribbon hanging in loose curls like a pig's tail. And on the paper was the picture of a mouse, standing on some straw, looking at a huge star shining in the sky.

Oscar had a closer look.

"He looks just like me!" he thought, as the mouse stared back at him. He climbed on to the package and carefully sniffed the paper.

Suddenly the parcel slid off the top of the pile and Oscar fell with it, clawing the paper to keep his balance. Oscar and the parcel landed heavily on the floor. Oscar stood still, ears pricked, listening. Silence.

Then he turned to look at the parcel and his heart sank. His claws had made large holes in the paper. In desperation Oscar pulled the ribbon with his teeth and tried to cover the largest tear, but it was no good.

He put his head inside the parcel and burrowed around like a mole. It was dark in there, but his eyes were used to the night.

"This," he said firmly, "must be a book. It must be a book for mice as it has a picture of a mouse on it. I am a mouse, so it must be a book for me!"

So Oscar began to open the parcel. He ripped back the paper, nibbled through the ribbon and stood on the cover of the book.

There were letters on the front, large, black letters, which Oscar could not read. He stood by the side of the book and began to push his head under the cover.

Easing his body forward, Oscar slid like liquid under it. He straightened his back and felt the cover swing open like a door.

Then, to his surprise, he lost his balance and felt himself falling, twisting and turning, head over tail until... he landed and lay still, eyes closed, body shaking.

A warm breeze ruffled his fur and Oscar opened one eye.

The tree, the glitter and the parcels had vanished. Oscar saw straw and hay and smelt the familiar smell of cows and sheep. The straw made his nose tickle and he sneezed.

"Atishoo!"

"Shh!" said a voice behind him. Oscar jumped. "Shh!" said the voice again. Oscar turned round and there, standing behind him, was a small, brown mouse.

"Hello," said Oscar cautiously. "Do you think you could tell me where..."

"Shh!" repeated the mouse. "Look!" he whispered, and he pointed to something beyond the hay.

Oscar blinked as his eyes became accustomed to the dim light. He could just see the figures of two human beings huddled together.

"What's happening?" he whispered.

"I'll tell you in a minute," replied the mouse.

"Waaahhh!" A small cry went up and the figures moved.

"It's a baby!" exclaimed Oscar. He watched as the man gently put his arm around the woman.

"Isn't he beautiful, Joseph?" she said, rocking the baby in her arms. The man smiled and nodded. "Yes, Mary," he said. "He's beautiful."

"And now," said the mouse, tapping Oscar on the shoulder, "allow me to introduce myself. I'm Matthew Mouse. Welcome! Sorry I was so rude, but something very special has just happened."

"I don't understand..." said Oscar, uncertainly.

"You're not from Bethlehem, are you?" asked Matthew. "A visitor, I suppose?"

"Yes, I'm a visitor. At least, I think I'm a visitor," said Oscar. "I'm Oscar from... well, from Book actually!"

"Book? Never heard of it. But anyway, you're most welcome!"

"Thank you," said Oscar. "I've had quite a night!"

"Haven't we all! God promised us that this would be a very special night, and it's not over yet."

19

"Who?" said Oscar.

"Why, God, of course!" said Matthew. "You know who God is, don't you?"

Oscar looked blank.

"Why, God!" continued Matthew, amazed. "God who made everything – the world, the stars, the planets, the trees, the people, the cows, the dogs, the sheep, the cats..."

"Cats?"

"Yes, cats – and mice," added Matthew. "He made everything. But you must be hungry. Come with me now and have something to eat."

Oscar scurried behind Matthew, until they reached the furthest corner. Oscar saw a small hole in a pile of hay.

"Home!" said Matthew proudly. "Come and eat!"

Oscar sank on to the floor of the mouse hole and sighed.

"Are you all right?" asked Matthew. Oscar nodded wearily.

"Thank you," he whispered, as Matthew pushed a large grain of wheat towards him. The food made him feel better and he began to relax.

"Feeling better?" asked Matthew cheerfully.

"I can't remember when I last had something to eat!" said Oscar. And he started to tell Matthew all that had happened, the cat, the boot, the beautiful room and finally the book.

Matthew listened intently, his eyes growing bigger and bigger, and his mouth opening wider and wider. When Oscar had finished he let out a slow, long whistle.

"What a story!" he said.

"Yes," said Oscar gloomily. "I won't blame you if you don't believe me. It's all so incredible."

"Oh, I believe you!" said Matthew, giving Oscar a hearty slap on the back. "After all, incredible things sometimes happen."

"Do they?" replied Oscar. "They never happen to me. At least, not until now."

"Well," said Matthew, rubbing his hands with excitement, "what's happened here tonight is more incredible than what's happened to you."

"I thought babies were born every day."

"That's true," said Matthew thoughtfully, "but this baby is a special baby. This baby is Jesus, God's only son, and God has given him to the world as a gift, a present!"

Matthew paused. "Listen!" Four ears strained to hear muffled sounds. Suddenly Matthew took Oscar firmly by the neck and pulled him out of the hole. All around them were stamping hooves, while the air was filled with the sound of bleating sheep.

"Watch it!" shrieked Matthew, as a large hoof moved towards them.

"Up the top! Climb to the top!" he shouted, and he pushed Oscar to the top of a large bale of hay.

Oscar sat and watched shepherds carrying crooks and slings, panting as if they had hurried there, and everywhere the noise of bleating animals.

Mary moved towards the manger which she had made
into a cradle. She bent down to pick up the baby.

There was a hushed silence as one by one the shepherds
sank to their knees.

"The angel was right," whispered one to another. "This
baby is the Saviour of the world."

He turned to Mary and Joseph. "We saw an angel," he
explained, "out in the fields. He said if we came to
Bethlehem we would find a baby in a manger."

"At first we were terrified!" said another. "One moment it
was pitch dark, the next there was a shining light, brighter
than the sun. Then there was a voice telling us not to be
afraid."

"When I heard the voice," continued the first shepherd, "I
looked up to see an angel, a messenger from God, and I
wasn't frightened any more."

Then in a jumble of excited words the shepherds told
their story of how from nowhere, the sky was full of angels,
all praising God, filling the night air with beautiful sounds.

"What did the angels sing?" asked Mary.

"They sang 'Glory to God in the highest, and peace to his people on earth,' " said the shepherds.

"Glory to God in the highest," repeated Mary and Joseph, "and peace to his people on earth!"

"Glory to God in the highest..." said Matthew.

"... and peace to his people on earth!" answered Oscar. The words filled him with warmth and happiness. "Glory to God!" he squeaked again from the top of the hay bale.

The stable was filled with the sound of singing. The melody and rhythm of the song filtered through every part of Oscar's body. He sang with all his might, his body moving with the music.

Eventually there was silence once more. No one moved. Oscar sat looking down at the little baby. At that moment he felt as if there were no one else in the world but himself and the baby. It was as if he had touched, heard, smelt, tasted and seen the most beautiful and exciting thing ever.

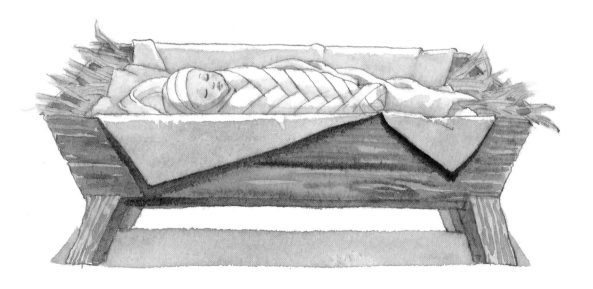

Then there were sounds again. The shepherds stood up and left the stable. As each one left, he looked at the little baby as if he were sorry to leave him. Soon there was no one left but Mary, Joseph and the baby.

The dawn light gently glowed under the door. Oscar felt Matthew put a friendly arm around his shoulders.

"Wasn't that wonderful?" whispered Matthew.

Oscar nodded. "Now I understand," he said slowly. "This baby really is very, very special. Jesus can be God's present to everyone."

Matthew gave Oscar a squeeze. "Morning's coming!" he said. "We'd better make ourselves scarce!"

"Before we go," said Oscar, "do you think we can have a closer look?"

Matthew glanced at the scene below and nodded.

"Well," said Matthew as they climbed down the legs of the manger, "I think we'd better get going!"

"Where to?" asked Oscar.

"I've got some cousins who live down the road. I can't wait to tell them what we've seen tonight! You can come too, if you like. I'll just go back and get some grain to take to them. You go on ahead. Do you see that small hole in the corner? I'll meet you outside!"

Oscar nodded and scurried towards the hole. He started to squeeze through, pushing as hard as he could until finally he was on the other side.

But instead of being outside, Oscar was still in the dark.

"Matthew!" he called. "Matthew!" But it was no good. He felt himself being squeezed and pulled and tugged as he struggled and wriggled. He pushed with his head until suddenly... he was free.

Oscar blinked. The air around him felt cool, but he was not outside. He was sitting on top of the book, in the room with the tree and the tinsel and the shimmering decorations and bright balloons.

Oscar slowly moved off the open book and stared at the room.

"It's strange," he said aloud. "I thought this room was the most beautiful room I'd ever seen, but it's not nearly as special as the room with the manger and the baby!"

He looked up at the tree and saw the angel on the top. He glanced at the pictures round the room and saw some shepherds. He recognised them! He saw the faces of small choir boys, mouths open wide, singing joyfully, and he knew what they were singing!

"I know what all these decorations are for," said Oscar slowly. "This room has been decorated for a party, a party to celebrate what I've seen tonight, a party for the baby Jesus."

He saw again the open book and leapt towards it. There on the page was a picture of the shepherds, the sheep and Mary and Joseph. And under the manger were two small mice. But Oscar wasn't looking at them. He had his eyes fixed on the baby lying in the manger.

Oscar stared at the picture for a while. Then somewhere, from the innermost part of his body, came the words he had repeated that night.

"Glory to God in the highest," he shouted, "and peace to his people on earth!"

Very slowly, Oscar left the book. He moved towards the door and, taking one last look at the picture of the baby, left the room. Oscar tip-toed into the hall, crawled into the boot... and waited to be set free into the garden.

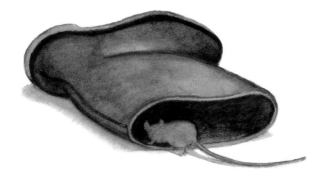

Copyright © 1992 AD Publishing Services Ltd
Text copyright © 1992 Stephanie Jeffs
Illustrations copyright © 1992 Jenny Thorne

A Tamarind Book
Published in association with SU Publishing
130 City Road, London EC1V 2NJ
ISBN 1 873824 03 3

First edition 1992

Printed and bound in Singapore